#26 Angeles Mesa
Branch Library
2700 W 52nd Street
Los Angeles, CA 90043

Te necesito, querido dragón

I Need You, Dear Dragon

por/by Margaret Hillert

Ilustrado por/Illustrated by Jack Pullan

NORWOOD HOUSE PRESS

Querido padre o tutor: Es posible que los libros de esta serie para lectores principiantes les resulten familiares, ya que las versiones originales de los mismos podrían haber formado parte de sus primeras lecturas. Estos textos, cuidadosamente escritos, incluyen palabras de uso frecuente que le proveen al niño la oportunidad de familiarizarse con las más comúnmente usadas en el lenguaje escrito. Estas nuevas versiones han sido actualizadas y las encantadoras ilustraciones son sumamente atractivas para una nueva generación de pequeños lectores.

Primero, léale el cuento al niño, después permita que él lea las palabras con las que esté familiarizado, y pronto podrá leer solito todo el cuento. En cada paso, elogie el esfuerzo del niño para que desarrolle confianza como lector independiente. Hable sobre las ilustraciones y anime al niño a relacionar el cuento con su propia vida.

Al final del cuento, encontrará actividades relacionadas con la lectura que ayudarán a su niño a practicar y fortalecer sus habilidades como lector. Estas actividades, junto con las preguntas de comprensión, se adhieren a los estándares actuales, de manera que la lectura en casa apoyará directamente los objetivos de instrucción en el salón de clase.

Sobre todo, la parte más importante de toda la experiencia de la lectura es ¡divertirse y disfrutarla!

Dear Caregiver: The books in this Beginning-to-Read collection may look somewhat familiar in that the original versions could have been a part of your own early reading experiences. These carefully written texts feature common sight words to provide your child multiple exposures to the words appearing most frequently in written text. These new versions have been updated and the engaging illustrations are highly appealing to a contemporary audience of young readers.

Begin by reading the story to your child, followed by letting him or her read familiar words and soon your child will be able to read the story independently. At each step of the way, be sure to praise your reader's efforts to build his or her confidence as an independent reader. Discuss the pictures and encourage your child to make connections between the story and his or her own life.

At the end of the story, you will find reading activities that will help your child practice and strengthen beginning reading skills. These activities, along with the comprehension questions are aligned to current standards, so reading efforts at home will directly support the instructional goals in the classroom.

Above all, the most important part of the reading experience is to have fun and enjoy it!

Shannon Cannon

Shannon Cannon, Ph.D., Consultora de lectoescritura / Literacy Consultant

Norwood House Press • www.norwoodhousepress.com
Beginning-to-Read ™ is a registered trademark of Norwood House Press.
Illustration and cover design copyright ©2018 by Norwood House Press. All Rights Reserved.

Authorized Bilingual adaptation from the U.S. English language edition, entitled I Need You, Dear Dragon by Margaret Hillert. Copyright © 2017 Margaret Hillert. Bilingual adaptation Copyright © 2018 Margaret Hillert. Translated and adapted with permission. All rights reserved. Pearson and Te necesito, querido dragón are trademarks, in the US and/or other countries, of Pearson Education, Inc. or its affiliates. This publication is protected by copyright, and prior permission to re-use in any way in any format is required by both Norwood House Press and Pearson Education. This book is authorized in the United States for use in schools and public libraries.

LIBRARY OF CONGRESS CATALOGING-IN-PUBLICATION DATA
Names: Hillert, Margaret, author. | Pullan, Jack, illustrator. | Del Risco,
    Eida, translator.
Title: Te necesito, Querido Dragón = I need you, Dear Dragon / por Margaret
    Hillert ; ilustrado por Jack Pullan ; traducido por Eida Del Risco.
Other titles: I need you, Dear Dragon
Description: Chicago, IL : Norwood House Press, [2017] | Series: A
    beginning-to-read book | Summary: "Dear Dragon feels rejected when a new
    baby arrives. Love and reassurance put him at ease as he finds new ways to
    help with the new addition to the family. Spanish/English edition includes
    reading activities"-- Provided by publisher.
Identifiers: LCCN 2016053228 (print) | LCCN 2017014207 (ebook) | ISBN
    9781684040339 (eBook) | ISBN 9781599538341 (library edition : alk. paper)
Subjects: | CYAC: Babies--Fiction. | Dragons--Fiction. | Spanish language
    materials--Bilingual.
Classification: LCC PZ73 (ebook) | LCC PZ73 .H5572116 2017 (print) | DDC
    [E]--dc23
LC record available at https://lccn.loc.gov/2016053228

Hardcover ISBN: 978-1-59953-834-1   Paperback ISBN: 978-1-68404-020-9

302N—072017
Manufactured in the United States of America in North Mankato, Minnesota.

Aquí viene el carro.

Sí, aquí viene el carro.

Veo a mamá.

Mamá está en casa.

Here comes the car.

Oh, here comes the car.

I see Mother.

Mother is home.

3

Mamá, mamá.
Ya estás en casa.
Eso es bueno.

Mother, Mother.
Now you are home.
This is good.

¿Esa es la bebé?
Quiero verla.
¡Ay, quiero verla!

Is that the baby?
I want to see her.
Oh, I want to see her!

6

Oh, cielos.
Oh, cielos.
Una bebé pequeñita.

Oh, my.
Oh, my.
A little, little baby.

7

¡Qué bebé tan bonita!
Es una bebé bonita.
¡Mira, mira!

What a pretty baby!
What a pretty baby she is.
Look, look!

Aquí.
Aquí.
Aquí es donde vamos.

In here.
In here.
This is where we go.

Esto es algo para la bebé...

This is something for the baby—

y esto...

and this—

TALCO
PARA
BEBÉS

BABY
POWDER

12

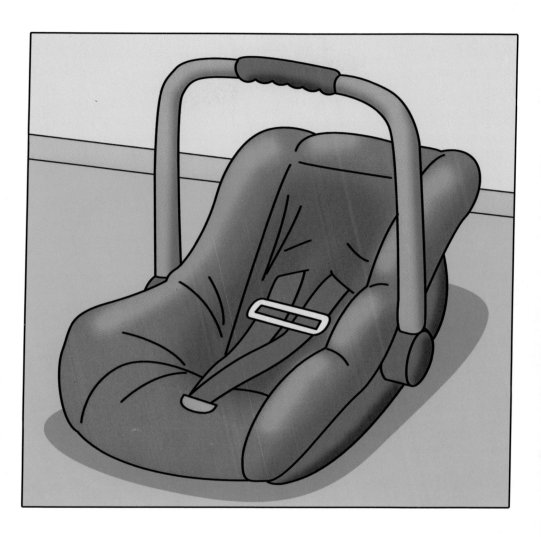

y esto.

and this.

Papá, papá.
¿Puedo cargar a la bebé?
Quiero cargar a la bebé.

Father, Father.
Can I have the baby?
I want the baby.

Caramba, qué bonita es.
Tan pequeñita, tan pequeñita.
Me caes bien, bebita.

My, what a pretty one.
So little, so little.
I like you, little baby.

Toma, mamá.
Es una bebita muy buena.
Me cae bien.

Here, Mother.
This is a good little baby.
I like her.

Ah, aquí estás.
No entraste.
Queremos que entres.

Oh, there you are.
You did not come in.
We want you to come in.

17

Mira.
Aquí hay algo que
se parece a ti.
Es para la bebé.

See.
Here is something
that looks like you.
It is for the baby.

A la bebé le va a gustar.
Sí, sí.
A la bebé le va a gustar.

The baby will like it.
Yes, yes.
The baby will like it.

Ven aquí.
Ven aquí.
Puedes hacer algo aquí.
Ven.
Ven.

Come here.
Come here.
You can do something here.
Come on.
Come on.

Mira ahora.
Mira lo que puedes hacer.
Es algo bueno que tú puedes hacer.

See now.
Look what you can do.
This is a good thing for you to do.

Mira eso.
Le caes bien a la bebé.
Y a mí también me caes bien.
De veras.
¡De veras!

Look at that.
The baby likes you.
And I like you, too.
I do.
I do!

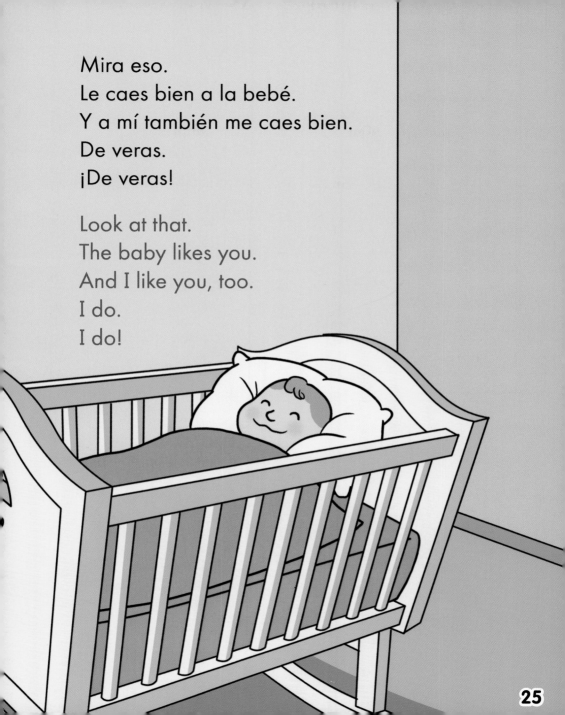

La bebé es pequeña.
Muy pequeña para jugar conmigo ahora.
Pero tú y yo podemos jugar.

The baby is little.
Too little to play with me now.
But you and I can play.

Podemos jugar y divertirnos.
Ven conmigo.
Ven a jugar.
¡Corre, corre, corre!

We can play and have fun.
Come on with me.
Come on and play.
Run, run, run!

Tú estás conmigo.
Y yo estoy contigo.
Te necesito.
Te necesito, querido dragón.

Here you are with me.
And here I am with you.
I need you.
I need you, Dear Dragon.

READING REINFORCEMENT

The following activities support the findings of the National Reading Panel that determined the most effective components for reading instruction are: Phonemic Awareness, Phonics, Vocabulary, Fluency, and Text Comprehension.

Phonemic Awareness: The /y/ sound

Oral Blending: Say the beginning and ending sounds of the following words and ask your child to listen to the sounds and say the whole word:

/y/ + ou = you	/y/ + es = yes	/y/ + ear = year
/y/ + am = yam	/y/ + arn = yarn	/y/ + uck = yuck
/y/ + ard = yard	/y/ + ellow = yellow	

Phonics: The letter Yy

1. Demonstrate how to form the letters **Y** and **y** for your child.
2. Have your child practice writing **Y** and **y** at least three times each.
3. Ask your child to point to the words in the book that have the letter **y** in them.
4. Write down the following words and ask your child to circle the letter **y** in each word:

yes	you	baby	my	funny
money	key	young	cycle	pretty
your	silly	cry	maybe	yard

Vocabulary: Adjectives

1. Explain to your child that words that describe something are called adjectives.
2. Say the following nouns and ask your child to name an adjective that might be used to describe it (possible answers in parentheses):

car (fast)	flower (pretty)	candy (sweet)
snake (slimy)	clown (funny)	sun (bright)
cotton (soft)	mansion (big)	ice (cold)

3. Ask your child to name the adjectives that might be used to describe babies. (Possible answers: pretty, tiny, cute, cuddly, sweet, soft, wiggly, little, chubby, noisy, etc.)

4. Write the words on separate pieces of paper.

5. Mix the words up and read each word aloud to your child. Encourage your child to explain how the adjective describes babies.

6. Mix the words up again and randomly say each word to your child. Ask your child to point to the correct word.

Fluency: Shared Reading

1. Reread the story to your child at least two more times while your child tracks the print by running a finger under the words as they are read. Ask your child to read the words he or she knows with you.

2. Reread the story taking turns, alternating readers between sentences or pages.

Text Comprehension: Discussion Time

1. Ask your child to retell the sequence of events in the story.

2. To check comprehension, ask your child the following questions:

- Where do you think the boy's mother and father were?

- What are the things the family has for the baby on pages 11–13?

- How does the boy feel about having a new baby in the family? How do you know?

- How does Dear Dragon help the baby?

- Do you think you would make a good big brother or sister? Why?

ACERCA DE LA AUTORA

Margaret Hillert ha ayudado a millones de niños de todo el mundo a aprender a leer independientemente. Fue maestra de primer grado por 34 años y durante esa época empezó a escribir libros con los que sus estudiantes pudieran ganar confianza en la lectura y pudieran, al mismo tiempo, disfrutarla. Ha escrito más de 100 libros para niños que comienzan a leer. De niña, disfrutaba escribiendo poesía y, de adulta, continuó su escritura poética tanto para niños como para adultos.

ABOUT THE AUTHOR

Margaret Hillert has helped millions of children all over the world learn to read independently. She was a first grade teacher for 34 years and during that time started writing books that her students could both gain confidence in reading and enjoy. She wrote well over 100 books for children just learning to read. As a child, she enjoyed writing poetry and continued her poetic writings as an adult for both children and adults.

ACERCA DEL ILUSTRADOR

Jack Pullan, ilustrador talentoso y creativo, es graduado de William Jewell College. También ha estudiado informalmente en la Universidad de Oxford y en el Instituto de Arte de Kansas City. Sus mentores han sido los renombrados acuarelistas Jim Hamil y Bill Amend. La obra de Jack ha adornado las páginas de numerosos y placenteros libros para niños, diversos materiales educativos y tiras cómicas, así como también muchas tarjetas de felicitación. Jack reside actualmente en Kansas.

ABOUT THE ILLUSTRATOR

A talented and creative illustrator, Jack Pullan, is a graduate of William Jewell College. He has also studied informally at Oxford University and the Kansas City Art Institute. He was mentored by the renowned watercolor artists, Jim Hamil and Bill Amend. Jack's work has graced the pages of many enjoyable children's books, various educational materials, cartoon strips, as well as many greeting cards. Jack currently resides in Kansas.